Jim Williams is a young man who always wanted to write. Having a vivid imagination and a flair for the dramatics helped him move forward with it, writing multiple stories that intertwine. Currently, he is studying English Literature in Aristotle University of Thessaloniki, hoping that someday he will reach a high academic level.

I dedicate this book to my dearest mother,
who supported me each step of the way!

Jim Williams

THE TALES OF HIDDEN TRUTH I

AUSTIN MACAULEY PUBLISHERS™

LONDON • CAMBRIDGE • NEW YORK • SHARJAH

A CIP catalogue record for this title is available from the British Library.

ISBN 9781528981835 (Paperback)
ISBN 9781528981842 (Hardback)
ISBN 9781528981859 (ePub e-book)

www.austinmacauley.com

First Published (2021)
Austin Macauley Publishers Ltd
25 Canada Square
Canary Wharf
London
E14 5LQ

Part One
Azure's Colourful Adventures

Chapter One
The Girl Named Azure

In a distant land, there was a kingdom that ruled the ground and sky. In that kingdom, there was a family that lived at the outskirts of the capital city. The house seemed rundown, but that was a deceit created by the family to keep away bandits. The family that lived there was happy. But that happiness did not last for long...

Well, I'm getting ahead of myself...In that little house lived a man and his wife, along with their two daughters. The two girls were beautiful, with golden hair and deep enigmatic eyes, they resembled their mother. The father was dark-haired (there was a son also, but I will not speak of his tale now).

But one day tragedy strokes this family and the elder daughter went missing, without leaving the slightest clue as to where she might've gone to. The mother and father were devastated with their loss and they couldn't do anything to find their daughter; so, they made sure that their one and only daughter, now, will have everything she ever desired.

So, little Azure (that was the name of the younger sister) became quite spoiled, that however, didn't mean that she was witless! She was extremely smart and creative. She could outsmart most (if not all) adults without even trying.

Little Azure adored her parents with all her heart. After all, they gave everything to her, and they did so without asking anything in return. Azure was truly happy. However, a time came when she felt uneasy. At the time she entered the teenage years (that was the age her sister had gone missing), she suddenly became somewhat worried of death and ageing.

She spoke to her parents about her worries, but they didn't take her too seriously, for she was too young to even think about old age and death. They also did not link that this fear had anything to do with the disappearance of their other daughter, for they somehow managed to block the whole event into the darkest corner of their minds.

So, Azure didn't have the support of any kind from anyone. Well, almost anyone...You see, dear Azure found a book in her father's study, an interesting book that told an interesting tale; a tale of an object that prevented one from ageing and from dying. And the moment she read about this tale, she became obsessed with it, wanting to find it.

There was, however, a complication with all this. She couldn't know if this tale was just a tale, or if there was truth in it. So, she had to do something about it...she had to ask her father; after all, she found the book in his study. So Azure, asked her father about the story, and she did it in a way that it wouldn't attract unwanted attention.

As expected, Azure, acquired the information she desired without attracting her father's suspicion. She had already made up her mind as to what she'll do next. She had to find that object, the legendary Dream flower.

Chapter Two

The Beginning of the Wondrous Adventure

Azure, prepared a small bag with provisions and she set out in secret. She sneaked in a carriage that was off to the place the first clue was located. You see, the tale of the legendary Dream flower was like this:

"In some faraway lands,
There are flowers that show the way,
They show the truth, the beauty, the sorrow, the joy, These flowers shield one from fear and hate,
And they pour-in colour, in the colourless lives that surround them.
There is, however, a flower that is different from the rest,
The effects of this flower are not confined in the boundaries of this world,
It hides in a cave that is one with the night-sky, the cave that is dyed in silver,
And it grants the most elusive and wondrous power of all,
It veils the holder with a mystical glow and shields him from Death and age...But be warned!

One cannot find that flower of dreams that easily,
One can find it only if willing to travel to distant lands and
bypassing all kinds of dangers,
Bravery is not the only virtue one must possess to attempt
this journey,
Wits of high level are also required.
The first clue, in finding this special flower, is located in a
distant land, near the Deep-Blue Lake.
In order for one to reach the cave, one must first reach this
lake, for one must find the first clue, if that one desires to
know the
Location of the next.
Oh, and one final warning,
O you who will try obtaining this flower,
Keep in mind this also: it's true that this flower will keep
You young and beautiful forever, veiling you from death…
But never forget that it could also veil you, and protect You
from something else, other than your fears.
The last thing I have to tell you is this, your prize is called,
The Dream Flower,
Good luck."

Azure did not take her father's book with her, because she
memorized this tale. And this tale was the only thing twisting
inside her head, nothing else.

Many days passed and she was still on the same
carriage; but not as a thief, as a guest of honour. You
see, the owner of the carriage went back to check his
merchandise and he saw Azure sleeping there. Instead of
waking her up or raise a ruckus, he carefully took the child
into his arms and carried her inside the carriage.

12

This man was an honest and good man. His heart was pure, so he couldn't possibly do any harm to the young girl. He patiently awaited her to wake up and find out who she was.

When Azure finally woke up, she was startled. She didn't expect to wake up inside the carriage. She calmed down after the honest man explained to her the situation.

Azure thanked him with a smile; she looked like the shining sun when she smiled and this smile was completely sincere, for if it wasn't, this man would know. He may have been a man of low status, but he possessed many powers.

He asked her name and her purpose. And he did it in such a nice manner that no one would've refused to answer him. Even if Azure wanted to conceal her name and purpose, she would've told him anyway.

But the truth is that Azure didn't have any intention of lying to him. She told him everything and when I say everything, I mean everything. She told him her story, all the tales of her life, even though he did not ask for them.

The most surprising part of this encounter was that this nice man actually listened to the whole thing without interrupting her; and he listened with a genuine care and attention. He seemed somewhat interested in her story. But in his eyes, there was no shadow, no negative thought was shown, even when he heard about her purpose, about the prize she set out to seek.

The only emotion that veiled his eyes was sorrow. The first veil appeared when she spoke of her sister and as to how her parents forgot about her, and the second and thickest veil appeared when she said that she wanted the 'Dream Flower'.

The man smiled at the end of her story and gave her water and bread, to drink and eat. He then, introduced himself with high manner. His name was Silver. He said nothing else. He just gazed outside the window while sorrow was still veiling his eyes.

Azure noticed that sorrowful look; she noticed it from the very beginning, from the time that it first appeared. And she felt strange about it...she felt strange about that man too, she wasn't afraid of him, and she felt that she could trust anything to him. Somehow, he felt familiar.

When she finished eating, she dared to do something that she hadn't attempted to do even to her father...she embraced Silver. He was happy that she did it. He embraced her back with a broad smile. She felt comfortable and immediately she fell asleep. Azure never attempted to give her father a hug after the disappearance of her sister.

Azure awoke the next day, and when she did, Silver was fast asleep. She didn't move, she waited for him to wake up. Of course, fate had something else in store for her. A terrible storm came out of nowhere. There were moments that she felt terrified; however, they were only moments...

She braced herself immediately and decided to act. She steered the horses towards the right. She saw at the map beside her that there was a cave close to them. They had to get there for cover, for if they were to stay out in the open, they would surely perish.

Thanks to her quick-thinking and bold moves, they reached the cave safe and sound. When they did, Silver woke up; and yet, he wasn't surprised in the least...one would think that he would at least bud an eyelash for that detour, but! He was perfectly fine with the sight he was seeing. It was like he knew that...

Azure was surprised by his attitude...she expected him to yell at her for not taking him up and then blame her for the storm. Instead, he only smiled to her, and to top that off, he thanked her for saving them.

It was strange for Azure to hear that she had just saved them. He meant the horses too, but she was late for that uptake...Silver really stole her heart. She saw him like the older brother that she never had, and the father she wished to have...

Silver sat down and nodded that she should do the same. But this time Azure was surprised nearly to a shocking point, for this time Silver's face was serious, and it was terrible to behold.

Azure sat down mesmerized by Silver's sudden change. Silver was really serious, but not mean, he congratulated her for her actions and gave her directions for her quest. She couldn't believe her ears...this was all a test...Silver was actually testing her...

"I must tell you...if you had failed, I would take you back to your home, to your parents!" he told her, "But you proved yourself to be able to take care of yourself in tough situations, and of them, you'll find plenty!"

Azure was happy to hear that. She actually received a vote of confidence from someone. Her parents thought of her to be a helpless child, never admitting that she's smarter than them. But that happiness was nearly disappeared, after she heard that they had to part ways...

Silver told her that it was time for them to part after the storm would pass. He said that he'd give her one horse, out of the four he had, but she'd have to release it, when she reached the Lake.

Silver told her to be careful, and sang her a song for a farewell.

"Your name defines the sky,
It gives the sea its light,
It grants the moon a mighty glow,
To shine the darkness of the night,
But as it does that, your name darkens,
And it waits a certain power to spring up,
So that it can be once again complete and mild,
The sun warms the sky, and your name restores and flies,
Across the world, it goes,
Through grass, and fire, and ice,
It reaches waterfalls of old,
That flow endlessly through land,
Flowing through, flowing through,
Boundless and free, it goes with thee,
To find the one thing that all desire,
Free of chain, free of fear, free of all things that could Ruin
everything you hold dear."

Silver sang that song for Azure. It was a strange song, but somehow Azure felt like she knew it, like she heard it somewhere before. But nonetheless, she loved it. After all, this song was talking about her name.

The storm passed and Silver stood up. Azure did the same. She was sad, she didn't want to say goodbye. Silver embraced her with a smile, trying to make her feel better, since he knew that this goodbye was hard for her.

Azure wept, and her tears were like stars, falling from her endless blue eyes. Silver kissed her forehead and said to her, "There is no need for you to be this sad, for this maybe is a goodbye, but it certainly isn't a farewell! If you truly believe it, and most importantly, want it, we will definitely meet again!"

Azure smiled, and her smile was that of the sun; and the whole cave was illuminated by the warmth of her smile. She embraced once again Silver with all her might, and then she mounted up (with Silver's help) the horse.

Silver once again warned her of the dangers that lie ahead, without of course being precise, not in the least; his warnings were vague and misty, only saying that she would be tested by this entire journey.

His final words to her in this tale were, "Good luck young one! Until we meet again!" then he commanded his horse to take her to the Lake. The horse heeded the command right away, while Azure was trying to look back, to take a last glimpse of the one person that came into her life and really understood her, without asking anything in return; the one person that truly felt like family.

Chapter Three
The Road to the Deep-Blue Lake

As the distance between her and Silver grew, Azure's tears were falling endlessly. She finally stopped looking back after it was impossible to even locate the place she was at before.

The horse that she was riding was silver colour. Well, all of Silver's horses had silver fur. It was majestic, and incredibly beautiful. It was riding smoothly and quite fast. Azure did not know its name, so she gave it a name, and strangely enough it responded to it. She named it Moonshine.

As they were riding on ahead, they passed through mountain and rivers, and lakes and towns (they didn't enter a town) and they all seemed small and distant.

It took a few days to cross the borders of the land, and get to the land she was seeking to go to. The land she was from was beautiful, but the land she just had gone to, was taking the word beautiful to a much higher level. Everything was green, the hills, the mountains, and even the rocks had growth on them. The animals there were free, and happy and big.

They passed through many lakes as they went. But since Moonshine did not stop, Azure figured that they hadn't arrived just yet. And she was right. The lakes they passed through were nothing compare to the Deep-Blue Lake she was searching for.

The lake was wide and it seemed to go really deep... Azure mounted down from Moonshine, and she kissed it on the head while saying, "We'll meet again for sure, dear Moonshine, go back to your master now and wait for me!" Moonshine neighed loudly and it was off, and was like a shooting star going out on a straight line.

Azure smiled and faced the lake. She was mesmerized by its beauty. The moon was reflecting on the centre of the lake. It was a full moon. But besides all this excitement she felt, she also felt uneasy, for she did not know as to how and where she was going to find the clue she needed to carry on her quest.

Chapter Four

The Deep-Blue Lake and the White Unicorn

It was midnight and Azure felt helpless. She didn't know where to start; she didn't have any information to the exact whereabouts of the clue. It was obvious to her that it was a bad idea to dive into the lake. For one, she didn't know how to swim...and second, she felt like this lake had no bottom.

Apparently, in this land such conditions of nature were normal, or it's the lake itself that had this treat, and as such it was called the Deep-Blue Lake. She gazed around the lake and she felt great. The greenery was rich, full of yellow flowers, some big, some small, and all of them had different shapes, the only feature they had in common was colour and beauty, they were all beautiful.

As she searched for hints to find the clue, she saw many interesting sights. There was a well near the lake; the water was probably from the lake. When she saw it, she suddenly felt extremely thirsty. It was an irresistible feeling, she couldn't help herself.

She walked towards the well, like a sleepwalker, she felt to be in a dream. When she reached the well, she bent over and looked down; there was pitched-black darkness inside the well, and it seemed that it went on forever as well.

There was a stir inside the well, and then a loud noise was heard. That noise was caused by a creature that jumped out of the water. Azure fell backwards; she got very startled by this. The creature stepped on the well and it could be clearly seen in the moonlight. It was a creature of the sea, human-like creature, like a merman, only much scarier, and seemingly more dangerous.

The moment that creature saw Azure, it smiled. It seemed somehow pleased from the young sight it had in front of it. Then it spoke, "Tell me, child, do you wish to drink from the water that lies in this well?"

Azure did not respond, for she could not find the willpower to do it. However, the thing that prevented her to speak wasn't fear…it was something else…

"Why are you not answering? Could it be that you are afraid of me?" the creature asked Azure with a pleasing attitude.

"I am not scared of you…" said Azure, causing the creature great shock, "You look lame…"

"WHAT?" the creature screamed, shattering the complete silence in the area, then it laughed and its face hardened. "Very well then… if that's how you want it…very well…"

"I don't understand you…" Azure told the creature and caught its attention once again, "By the way, what are you?" she also asked it. Rude, I know, but still, that's what she asked.

The creature's face hardened even more and it said, "What I am is of no concern to you, at least at this point. Now

21

you must know the consequences of attempting to drink water from this well."

"Why are there consequences in drinking water, no, why are there consequences in attempting to drink water from this well?" Azure asked the creature and stood up.

"How naïve…don't you know that the water of this well is the water of the lake beside it? No one is allowed to drink, unless if that one manages to defeat the creatures that live in there. But, you were lucky. How you ask? Well, you didn't try drinking of the lake, but only from this well. But nonetheless a crime it is. So the only options you have are, either to defeat me, or reason with me."

"How can I reason with you? You're clearly a savage beast…" Azure said to the creature.

The creature became angrier after that last comment, but it didn't snap. It only said, "Well, there is a way to reason with me, little girl. I will tell you a riddle and you must answer it. If you do, not only I'll let you drink, but I will not hurt you, not in the least. But fail, and I will kill you in the most painful way possible."

"Whatever…just tell me the riddle…" Azure told the creature.

The creature smiled broadly and then began speaking. And to Azure's great surprise, the language the creature spoke was unknown to her…she couldn't understand a thing… it was a trap!

The creature stopped talking and a broad smile decorated its ugly face. "Well? What's your answer? Now it's time for you to give it, unless of course, you want to hear the riddle again…" said the creature while it was barely able to control its laughter.

Azure's heart became cold after this deception. She knew nothing of the language, so there was no point in hearing it again.

"Am I to take this stunned silence as…? What? You don't know the answer, huh…you know the consequences for that…" said the creature and took a stance to strike Azure.

Humph, well, at least it tried…

A white flash illuminated the darkness of the night, and the creature withdrew backwards in fear; that flash was immensely strong, so strong that it scorched the creature's hands and half its face.

The creature screamed in pain and anger. Azure did not move, she just looked backwards to find the source of this light. What she saw did not surprise her, but she was certainly impressed to gaze such a beast, it was a Unicorn, a White Unicorn!

"You fowl creature, how dare you cheat this young girl!" said the unicorn to the creature.

"Stay out of this, Unicorn! This doesn't concern you! This brat sinned, she has to be punished!" said the creature to the unicorn.

"You are the sinner here, fool! You better stay away from her, or you'll pay the price!" said the Unicorn.

The creature did not give heed to Unicorns words and attacked Azure. Azure once again did not move, she only closed her eyes. And she was right to do so, for if her instincts hadn't guided her, she would have lost her sight. The White Unicorn shined bright, so bright that it incinerated the creature completely.

Then Azure and the Unicorn had a pleasant chat. Azure thanked it for saving her, and the unicorn introduced itself, its name was Unicorn (I know, lame...). Then Azure asked for information about the clue. And she was in luck, for this unicorn knew about it.

"Follow the white trail,
And you will find the colour that doesn't stick,
And when you do, think,
Where does this colour belong?
If you find the correct answer,
You will find the location of the next clue."

That's what Unicorn said to Azure. Azure thought of it a little. Then she had an idea about that small riddle. She asked the unicorn in a very polite manner to lead the way to that, colour that didn't stick.

The Unicorn neighed loudly and turned around galloping lightly. Azure followed, and she was quite pleased with her intellectual prowess in finding the correct answer.

The unicorn stopped. And when Azure finally caught up with it, she saw where it stopped. It stopped above a red flower! The words of that unicorn were true; indeed, the colour of that flower didn't stick in that garden.

But still, this didn't really explain the rest of the riddle. She did follow the white trail, and she did found the colour that didn't stick. But she didn't know as to how this will let her know the location of the next clue.

"I'm impressed with you, Azure," said the Unicorn, "You were able to figure out half the riddle without even trying, but I'm afraid that unless you know of many lands, you will never fully solve it."

"What do you mean?" Azure asked.

"It's quite simple, really. What you're searching for isn't in this land. It's located in a faraway land. A land that would take a normal horse years and years to reach," answered the Unicorn.

"Oh, my…" Azure sighed, "can you give me more details, please?"

"Of course, I can," the Unicorn neighed. "You see, this flower doesn't belong in this land, in fact, it belongs in a faraway land, in a land where the 'Wild Red Roses' bloom."

"I see…" said Azure and plunge into a deep thought; then after some moments, she said, "And you said that it would take a normal horse many, many years to reach that land, huh? How long would it take you?"

"Me? Hah, I can get there within five days. After all, you can't compare me with a common horse, for I am a Unicorn!" said the Unicorn, and its chest was fuelled with pride.

"I see. So, would it be much if I were to ask you to take me there? After all, you can take me there in no time at all," said Azure.

"Hmm, take you there, huh? Well, you did ask for it nicely, and I have nothing else to do…well, why not? I'll take you there, it might be fun." said the Unicorn.

Azure thanked it and hopped on. Then, she rode on the unicorn with the Wild Red Rose at hand, and she had rejoiced for her luck since luck seemed to be on her side; she rode on without looking back, back at the garden she had just left, the garden of yellow flowers that was burning.

Chapter Five
The Garden of Wild Red Roses

Azure travelled truly fast, while riding the unicorn. She felt incredibly good while riding, and the journey was pleasant, thanks to Unicorn's gentle galloping. She saw many great sights on the way; while she was crossing the borders of the land she was in, she noticed that the land she had just entered was really different from the one she had just left.

This land was full of mountains and hills, other tall, other short. The plant life was rich, different from the lands she'd seen. The plants, flowers, and trees were all over the hills and hilltops. Around the mountains were only tall trees, trees that were bearing fruit; fruits of strange shape.

Azure was amazed as to how the lands differ from one another. All of them were beautiful and unique. As she rode on, she saw many kinds of animals, mostly birds and horses. For a few seconds they went on par, but they couldn't keep up with the Unicorn's great speed.

She reached her destination, in just four days. And her amazement continued. She faced a wide field. The grass was green, beautiful, and while flowers were few, they were very beautiful. The flowers were getting more and more in number, as she rode on to reach the foot of the mountain, where the colour red was intense.

At the halfway there, something unexpected happened. A terrible screech sounded from the sky; and when they looked up, they saw a big and terrible eagle with big long wings. The eagle was circling down, with its eyes fixed on them.

"Who dares, to trespass my domain?" said the eagle with a loud and clear voice when it landed.

Azure explained her situation to the eagle, and when she did, the eagle told her that it'd help her. The eagle told her that it liked her, and for that, it would tell her the only way to get what she wanted. She had to know a little song.

When the eagle finished explaining something bizarre happened. It morphed, and got smaller and changed into a human…Well, something like human…it was a human-like at least. Its hands and back were covered with feathers. Then it recited the song:

"Roses are red, the sky is blue,
Will you please help me find
What I'm searching for?
In this world of colours, I need the one,
The one that will lead me onto the fabled colour,
The one that changes light, and darkness, and life, and for
me to find that, I really need the one,
I really need you clue,
In desperation, you're the one that's true."

After listening to it, Azure asked the eagle if this would really work. The eagle answered, "Of course." But Azure insisted on it, saying, "Is it really enough for me to just ask the clue to help me?"

After that question, the eagle turned its head towards Azure and smiled with its eyes closed, and then it said, "Sometimes, all you need to do is ask…"

And there they were, besides the Wild Red Roses and began singing all together the verse the eagle had told them…

However…

The Unicorn got confused, and at the fourth line it screwed it up…it mumbled something else, and when it did the roses stirred, like a wave of ice-cold chill just went through them.

A second later a loud noise was heard and big roots came out of the ground and they tried to capture the three companions. The Unicorn pushed Azure out of the way, and it got captured, as a result of that Azure escaped, barely. The eagle flew up; with blinding speed, it changed its form again.

Azure retreated backwards after the unicorn told her to, and she began brainstorming as to how she'll get out of this situation. Her main purposes were to take down this creature that appeared before her, find the clue and save the Unicorn.

She stared down the creature with her blue eyes. This adversary was actually a rose. A humongous Wild Red Rose, with its roots outside the ground, using them as hands, only instead of fingers it had thorns.

Apparently, it couldn't see a thing, but it seemed that it was able to smell, or somehow sense their presence. Somehow she had to defeat it, but it was a great challenge, for it was really difficult to get close enough to even damage it. Its roots were shielding it effectively.

And then it hit her! A great idea as to how she was going to defeat this Rose. She summoned the eagle to the ground to explain her plan, and when she did, her plan immediately got underway.

She closed into the dangerous flower, too close, actually, and as she had anticipated the flower was aware of her right away. And it attacked her with all of its roots. Azure dodged the incoming attack with unexpected agility, and when she did the flower became enraged, it forgot for a second the Unicorn and let a little loose the hold on it. A big mistake indeed, for the Unicorn is a divine beast, and it's not an easy task to capture it, especially with a half-hearted resolve.

But as she expected it wasn't enough just to weaken the hold, she had to shatter it. When the Rosie was busy in chasing after Azure, the eagle swooped down and tried in slicing the roots that held the Unicorn captive. It succeeded with its third try, and that was, maybe, the greatest thing of that day, for at that exact moment Azure fell down and the Rosie had almost 'hugged' her.

Well, almost…

The instant the Unicorn was free, it flashed right in front of Azure, and it scorched the Wild Red Flower. Azure was safe and the Unicorn thanked her for saving it, Azure, of course, didn't say anything, for she was the one that was saved first.

Then she bypassed the flaming remnants of the Wild Red Rose that tried to kill them and approached the normal roses, so that she can find the clue. And in her despair, she began chanting the song alone, with an incredibly melodic voice:

"Roses are red, the sky is blue,
Will you please help me find
What I'm searching for?
In this world of colours, I need the one,
The one that will lead me onto the fabled colour,
The one that changes light, and darkness, and life,
And for me to find that, I really need the one,
I really need you clue,
In desperation, you're the one that's true."

And when she finished, once again a shiver passed through all the roses, and a weak voice was heard asking who woke it up...

Do you know what it was? Do you know to whom this voice belonged to? Well, I tell you, if you thought a human-like eagle was weird, you would be extremely surprised to hear this...The voice belonged to a rose. But that rose was...well; it was just like the eagle, human-like! It had a human-like form, a form of a small child.

It asked her what she wanted.

Then once again, Azure, explained her situation.

Surprisingly, the young Wild Rose was oh-too-eager to help her; in fact, it actually offered her help on one condition...to take it with her.

Azure happily agreed on that one. Then the eagle announced to Azure that it would join her to, if she would allow it, saying, "You are going to need assistance from someone with keen eyes." Azure accepted the eagle as well.

Then off she was again, riding the Unicorn, while the rose and the eagle soared above them. The rose told Azure that the next clue was located in a forest in a faraway land; it was called 'The Legendary Golden Woods'.

And off she was, riding towards that legendary forest, the forest was the third clue located, the clue she desperately needed in order to find her prize, the Dream Flower.

Chapter Six

The Legendary Golden Woods

Azure reached the Golden Woods like the wind, fast and smooth. She passed through the neighbouring village, before entering the forest. The people there warned them not to enter that forest, because according to their legends something evil had rooted in there. But no one knew what it was.

Azure, of course, was very interested in their stories and she asked them to tell her some. What they told her threw her in dismay. The stories were nasty; she figured, of course, that some of their telling's were somewhat overblown, either because they wanted to scare her off for her safety, or maybe just because from mouth to mouth the story became quite fictitious.

But nevertheless, even if half of what they told her was true, it would be really hard for them to even survive this forest, let alone obtaining the clue. And once again she found herself in front of a difficult decision, to enter and go for it, or to go back…

She did take into account everything that happened up to that point in her journey, including her 'trip' with Silver, but still, she couldn't make up her mind. Thankfully, the villagers, who had taken a liking to her, gave her a room to sleep in, and food and water. They always hoped that they'll manage to persuade her to stay away from that forest, for she was young. That's why they made it easy for her in the village.

Azure stayed in the village for a week. She brainstormed like crazy, trying to reach a conclusion. She saw the villagers trying more and more to convince her not to enter into that forest, and somehow that was giving her strength. Then she remembered Silver and his words, "I would've taken you back, if you hadn't proven yourself in this tough situation…"

Afterwards, she felt confident enough to at least attempt entering into the forest. The whole village shivered in fear as to how the young girl will manage to survive this ordeal.

But Azure wasn't witless! What she really wanted to do was to get close enough so that she can see anything that could prove useful, while inside the forest. That way, she could devise a good plan, a plan that would limit the danger as much as possible.

And so she did. She approached the forest, and when she did, she smelled something nice. A nice scent was all over the woods. Somehow this feeling she just had, felt familiar…

She resisted into going in and ran towards the village. The villagers were happy about it. They thought that she came to her senses. That night Azure asked them, in the cleverest way possible, many things about that forest.

She asked them about that scent and of the 'darkness' of that forest. Now, of that scent, the only thing they knew was that anyone who was unlucky enough to sniff it, entered the forest and never came out, and that it was really a wonder that she resisted it! They actually believed that she was special.

As of the darkness...well, they didn't really understand her question, which was really natural, for they weren't really educated people, they were simple farmers; they loved the earth, not the books.

Azure felt grateful towards these people, and to show off her gratitude towards them, she told them that she'll teach a group of them to read and to write. They accepted, but not really willingly. They didn't believe in wisdom. They believed in labour. Of course, she explained them that both were vital if they wanted to do more than surviving.

She taught a class of twenty. She handpicked them herself. There were some of them, of course, that didn't really had any desire to learn, so in a way she forced them... but they also didn't refuse her, for this was all to express her gratitude; and even though they had no education, they still had high manners, and they knew that refusing such a selfless act wouldn't be proper.

To everyone's great surprise, all twenty of her students were quick to learn and really apt to the 'changes' she was teaching them about, even those who didn't want to learn; for even though they didn't want to learn, they still did their best to learn.

Mostly her students were adults. In fact, there were only four children. But even the children learned everything at the exact speed rate as the older students.

She taught them to read and to write, all of them had become really good at both learning and teaching. As the main gift, she wrote them a book of their history. She wrote down pretty much everything they told her, that way the stories would pass down on to the next generations. And she made the book in a way for one to be able to add up more to it. That way more and more stories would be added there, until the time for the beginning of a second book would be necessary.

She stayed in that village for six months. Her companions stayed with her, enjoying the pleasures of being relaxed and free. Azure then had to say goodbye to the villagers, for it was once again the time for her to attempt in obtaining the clue.

Before leaving the village, she did two things. The first thing was to order them not to follow her into the forest no matter the circumstances. And the second was to give them a letter. She told them that this letter contained a story, and if they wanted, they could write it down to the book she had written for them. But, of course, she told them that it was their choice whether they'd write it or not.

Azure asked of the eagle to scout the forest from above, but no matter what it shouldn't go to the core of the forest. She advised it to stick to the entrance.

The eagle scouted, and then Azure rode in. The Unicorn did not go very fast, on Azure's command, for they didn't really know what they would find in there. Azure called that forest 'bizarre' and 'perilous'.

And she was right to call it so, for when they entered, she, once again, sniffed that strange scent. She, of course, resisted, and this time with ease, but the other two weren't so fortunate.

And thanks to that, she became certain of her hypothesis about that scent. She commanded the Unicorn, and the rose to snap out of it and after a second, a second that seemed a year to them, they snapped out of it. Of course, Azure's wisdom went far beyond that, so she told them that they didn't have much time to search, and they had to split up. And so they did.

They covered great ground, when each on his own. However…The young rose screamed, and that scream shattered the perfect silence that covered the whole forest. And after that scream, the forest itself stirred. Surprisingly enough, Azure was pleased, for she believed that she had found her clue, and all she had to do was to go to the screaming young rose. Apparently, the unicorn had the same idea with Azure. What they didn't know was that the rose's scream was for something else…

When Azure arrived at the place, she came face to face with a beast that she didn't believe that existed! It was a dragon-like lizard. No wings, big mouth, big horns, big feet, small hands, and really, really sharp teeth; teeth that seemed countless by the way…

And that didn't make sense to her, for she didn't see anything like that when she gazed inside the forest back then. Those thoughts were interrupted by the lizard…it bypassed the rose, and attacked Azure. She was saved by the unicorn in the last instant!

The Unicorn once again scorched the air around it, and then attacked the lizard with a ray of light. That attack had no effect whatsoever. Azure was at dismay after that, because if the Unicorn wasn't strong enough to take on their enemy, then who was?

Then Azure thought that it would be best if she knew as to what had taken place with the rose from the beginning. So she asked it what happened. The rose was too frightened to speak, but in the end it did; after all, when it looked into Azure's bright blue eyes, all fear and anxiety vanished from its young heart.

The rose told her everything. But Azure didn't really have any idea about that lizard. Then she decided to watch its battle with the Unicorn. She watched and watched, but nothing new sprang into her mind. But then...

She had an idea! A brilliant idea, so brilliant that she wondered as to why she hadn't thought of it earlier. She picked a rock and threw it at the lizards heard. And surprisingly enough, it worked!

The lizard turned around and looked at Azure completely enraged. Azure smiled, pleased with herself; after all, the almighty Unicorn couldn't land a hit, and yet she did it with a simple rock...

Then the lizard attacked Azure and the rose who was standing right next to her. Azure asked it to unleash its own scent from its petals, and the rose obeyed. And when the scent covered the lizard, the lizard seemed to be in pain, great pain.

Then Azure punched the lizard in the face. And for a great surprise for the rose and the Unicorn the lizard fell down. But when it did, it was no longer a lizard...it was a three-tailed fox! Small and cute it was.

Then Azure smiled and looked at the fox, which was perfectly fine, and said to it, "This was all you, right? Your power is to create illusions with that sweet scent!"

The fox was quite happy that Azure was talking to it. It nodded yes to her answer and then went to her feet and cuddled, you know, like a cat. Then Azure asked of it the clue that was said to be in that forest. The fox nodded towards the right. It was there, beside a humongous tree, a small blue flower.

Azure went and picked it up, and when she did, once again the entire forest stirred, and the scent was gone altogether. But something else must've awakened in there, and she had a bad feeling about it. And that feeling became worse after she heard the eagle's cries from the sky.

They made a run for it. She hopped on the Unicorn, and the Unicorn dashed like the wind and outside the forest. What she didn't realize when she was running away, was that besides the rose, the fox hopped on the unicorn too.

Azure got the point right away. The fox wanted to join her. She allowed it with a smile, saying, "The more we are, the merrier!"

And once again she rode off towards her destination, holding the final clue that she needed to find the Dream Flower. And now she was only one step away into obtaining it, one step away into finally being free of all the fears that haunted her. And she rode off towards the conclusion of her journey with good company, company that brought her happiness and joy.

Chapter Seven

The Cave of Thousand Moons

Azure reached her destination swiftly. She arrived at the legendary Cave of Thousand Moons. It was said that in this cave one could find the fabled Dream Flower, at least according to the fox.

Azure was mesmerized by the beauty of this cave. Of course, beauty and cave does not really match, however, the tunnels of this cave had something all other caves were lacking...and that something was 'special decorations'.

These decorations were diamonds that were springing out of the earth, blooming like flowers; some even had the shape of flowers; and the other decoration were actual flowers, flowers that could not be found in any other place in the world, the mysterious flowers called 'Lunar Flowers'.

The Lunar Flowers had a strange shape. Their leaves were somewhat spikey, and all of them had the exact same shape and colour, which was silver. But these flowers weren't mysterious because of their shape. They were mysterious because they were, somehow, able to store in them the moonlight and starlight.

The starlight that was stored in them wasn't able to glow as much as the moonlight, of course, but it was enough to light up the corridors of the cave. The moon was the one that was really able to light up the Lunar Flowers, and somehow these flowers were able to 'share' the moonlight and starlight they had absorbed with each other; and that's how the entire cave was always bathed in silver light.

The entrance of the cave was a strange one too. It wasn't really a normal entrance, you know, like a door; it was actually a hole on the ground, a hole that was getting deeper. But fortunately, this hole wasn't too steep, and because of that, they were able to descend without any trouble. The only problem with that entrance was that it was tough to find; the fox had to use its own unique senses in order to locate it.

As they were descending deeper and deeper into the cave, Azure felt restless. She was aware of the Dream Flower's presence, and she couldn't believe that she was actually this close in obtaining it. But even though she was overjoyed, she didn't abandoned her wits, for she knew it wouldn't be easy for her to even reach the Dream Flower, let alone obtaining it.

She was on-edge on the whole way down. She was on-edge so much that her companions got worried. But she calmed them down and asked them to have a watchful eye as well, which they did.

While she was descending deeper into the cave, she felt glad that she found such trustworthy and reliable companions, and she felt happy having them, now that she will finally have her prize.

While having these beautiful thoughts, the cave was hit by a mighty shock. Her companions were all quite distressed after that shock, finally realising that it wouldn't be easy to reach the prize; of course, she had just told them that.

She didn't run. First, she had to try figuring out as to where that shock came from. Was it a normal earthquake, or maybe a creature that would try and stop her? Either way, this shock was bad news to her, cause an earthquake can block her way, and a creature can do all sorts of nasty things, other than blocking her way.

She continued walking after a while of trying in listening for any clues as to what caused the shock. She didn't find any. It was really tough. The rose began emanating a scent that smelled awful, out of its fear. And in order for it to stop, Azure had to reassure it that it was safe with her. When she did calm the rose down, the scent that was emanating was sweet.

Then another shock stroke and the cave quaked, and this shock was stronger than the last one. And it was clear to Azure that it wasn't from natural causes, something was creating these shockwaves; and that something was doing them probably because she was approaching her destination.

This time she ran. And she ran as fast as she could. She had to reach her destination before that something manages to catch up with her. But as she ran, she came across something that escaped her. She came across a double-crossing. And she didn't know which corridor to choose.

Fortunately for her, she accepted the little fox to go with her. That fox had many special abilities, and all of them were stored inside its little tails. It used the tails as a compass, and the tails chose for her the corridor that was right.

She ran towards the direction the fox guided her with all her might. Another shock stroke and the cave once again quaked. And this time it was stronger than ever, but the fear it caused gave wings to her feet and ran like the wind.

As she ran, she didn't notice how much the corridor walls around her were changing. The Lunar Flowers were increasing in number and the light was getting stronger, which was a beautiful sight indeed. And then...

Chapter Eight
The Crystal Lake

Azure had found herself in a wide space, like in a dream, beautiful and magnificently illuminated. She was looking at a lake, a lake inside this cave, the Cave of Thousand Moons. The lake was completely clean, one could see through the water like seeing through glass; around the lake were countless Lunar Flowers, all shining brightly, radiating a silver glow.

Well, the strangest thing about all this was the ceiling of this cave… you see, there was no ceiling. And because of that, the entire lake was bathed in the moonlight. Everything was illuminated; nothing was hidden from sight, all shadows fled in fear before the might of the moon.

Azure gazed around her. She couldn't believe her eyes. She couldn't believe that such beauty exists in the world. Everything in that place touched perfection. Mesmerizing beauty with no equal had taken root inside that cave. And by seeing this lake, she finally understood what made the Cave of Thousand Moons mysterious and legendary.

The flowers surrounding the lake were mostly Lunar Flowers, however, there were other kinds of flowers also; red flowers, blue flowers and some flowers, which their petals were dyed in two colours: the colours green and purple; these flowers, however, were few in number.

Near the lake, there was a shrine. The shrine was white and really beautiful…the shrine was actually quite plain, it was a massive rock, and all over it were carvings of flowers. The only two exceptions were a two-headed mermaid at the bottom and a text. The text said:

"There is Light deep within the Darkness,
A light that shines Silver, showing the way,
The way to the Crystal Lake,
The beautiful Crystal Lake with the clear cold water,
The water that sparkles in the moonlight,
In every sleepless night, the moon shines bright,
And it shows the path that leads to the Emerald Sanctuary."

This seemed familiar to Azure. She was certain that she had heard this one before. In her head sounded like a song, an opera-like song. And she couldn't explain why. She couldn't recall as to where she had heard it before…

Well, nevertheless, this text touched her soul. But, at the same, she felt uneasy. She didn't know what to do next. She had found the Crystal Lake, which apparently was the core of this cave, and at that point, she didn't know what to do. And in addition to all her worries, another one was added to the toll…what the hell was up with that two-headed mermaid…? Mermaids were supposed to be beautiful…

Azure began chanting the song, she thought that maybe there was a hidden meaning somewhere in there and it would be more obvious to her if the text was recited. Well, something did become obvious after the chanting of that text...

A screech shattered the silence of the night, a terrible screech that resounded to all the lands of the world. The moon's glow became weaker after that screech, to the point that it faded. Then the only sources of light were the Lunar Flowers, which fortunately for Azure, they shined brightly.

The lake became pitched black, worse than the Deep-Blue Lake...then another screech sounded, and it came from inside the lake. Then a pale glow appeared inside the Lake...and it moved fast, from one direction to the other, always closing in on them.

Azure moved fast, she picked up a Lunar Flower and threw it in the lake so that she can see what she was up against, although she already had a feeling as to what that was. And she was right! The enemy was the two-headed mermaid that was carved on that stone; only the real one was far more terrifying than the carving.

And once again it screeched terribly. Azure's eyes closed from the excruciating pain that the screech caused her. And the creature didn't lose time; it attacked her right away when her guard was down.

Fortunately for Azure, she wasn't alone; she had her friends with her. The fox used the power of one of its tails to throw off the mermaid's perception, causing it to miss. Then the next instant, the Unicorn unleashed a radiance targeting the mermaid. The mermaid was scorched, but not killed. It withdrew into the water.

And it was plainly obvious that it wasn't defeated either, for the moon was still hidden behind the veil of darkness the mermaid had summoned. But that veil was more dangerous than it first appeared to be. It swallowed the Unicorn's light almost immediately after it was released, and when the eagle prepared to take flight it was badly hurt by an unseeing foe, a foe that looked to Azure like it was the Darkness itself, so there was no point fighting it. As a result, of course, the eagle was badly hurt, being unable to help.

Then Azure had an idea inside the panic. She once again got near the Lake, knowing that the mermaid will try to get in the way. When she did the mermaid appeared again, but this time it didn't get out of the water. It was inside it and both of it mouths were grinning; then it spoken:

"You, who trespass, must return at once to where you came from; I shall give you this, one and only chance to withdraw. If you do choose to leave this place, I give you my word that you will leave the Cave of Thousand Moons safely; but should you deny my offer and choose to stay, it will be the last thing you'll ever do! If you stay, I promise that I will devour you all…!"

For Azure's great surprise she noticed that the burn caused by the Unicorn was gone, and the mermaid was completely healed. That meant that if she was to defeat that mermaid to get to her prize, she had to do it in one fell swoop.

She ignored the warning and told her friends of her plan and hypothesis about the mermaid. They all agreed to help her; the eagle was in bad condition, but it agreed too. The plan was simple. They had to illuminate the Lake, and then Azure would dive to search for any doorway or pathway that is hidden from her eyes.

And they did. They picked as many Lunar Flowers as they could, and threw them into the Lake. And of course, the plan worked; and it did like a charm! Not only the lake was illuminated, but the mermaid was nearly burned by the Lunar Flowers that made contact with it.

The mermaid's sudden weakening caused the Darkness to fade, almost completely, but the moon still did not shine. Regardless of the moonlight, this was the one and only opportunity that was presented to Azure. She had to grasp it. And she did. After all, her companions told her that it was time for her to get her prize. When they did, she dove into the lake with a Lunar Flower at hand.

There were many Lunar Flowers still glowing brightly inside the Lake. But the mermaid was still in there too. And its wounds were closing up rapidly. But still, it didn't dare to attack Azure with that many Lunar Flowers inside the lake, its plan was to wait to either lose their power, or to wait for Azure to run out of the air and attack her when she attempted to go for breath.

But Azure had other plans. She had no intention of dying or giving up. She was certain that somewhere inside this lake was a hidden doorway. And she was right. There was! However, there was a small problem. Well, the doorway was near the mermaid.

Azure didn't think much on it, she charged. The mermaid thought that she would tackle it and strike it with the Lunar Flowers, and because of that thought, it retreated in fear, giving the perfect opening for her.

She reached the entrance, but could not open it. Things looked bad, for she was nearly out of breath. The mermaid finally realized what just happened, and charged towards Azure with vengeance.

But once again fortune favoured little Azure. She had taken all the Lunar Flowers, while she swam towards that entrance. She held like eight of them. The moment that mermaid came near her, Azure flashed all eight of them right in front of its eyes.

As a result, the mermaid lost its sight, from all four eyes; and when it did, the doorway opened and sucked in Azure, but only Azure. The mermaid failed its mission to protect the Lake, so it was left behind, blind and plunged into fury.

Chapter Nine

The Dream Flower

Azure found herself into a hallway. She still held the Lunar Flowers, but they didn't have much light stored in them anymore. Most of it was used to blind the mermaid. So Azure figured that she had to move quickly, before her only source of light went out.

She began walking. In less than a minute, she found herself into another hallway, or maybe the same but a tad different. She no longer needed to worry about a source of light, for she had found it once again. In the entire hallway, Lunar Flowers were glowing, all shining brightly, which makes one to wonder as to how they manage to grow inside an underwater tunnel... oh well, the important thing was that Azure didn't need to worry anymore about the lights going out, for the Lunar Flowers that surrounded her shared their stored light with the dried up flowers she held, and then they were alive again, they looked fresh and strong, and more importantly, they were shining brightly with their usual beautiful silver glow.

She walked and walked. And finally, after some minutes, she arrived at her destination. The Emerald Sanctuary, in that chamber, it was like the stars themselves were raining, with the Lunar Flowers as the perfect theme. The ceiling was wide, and in the middle of it, there was a small hole, and somehow from it, the moonlight was shining down.

In the middle of this Sanctuary, there was a sight that would spellbind anyone. It was it. The fabled *Dream Flower*. And it wasn't rooted on the ground, no, it was floating on air, like there was a gentle breeze holding it enwrapped inside the moonlight, dazzling a mysterious light, with the colours of the rainbow at one moment, and the colour of the moonlight at the other.

Azure walked towards it slowly, with hypnotic steps, fearing that someone will attack her anytime now. But she was wrong! No one attacked her; no one appeared to prevent her from collecting her prize.

She picked it up.

And when she did all the orbs of light that surrounded her encircled her. Then they began forming words:

"Now that you have found your prize,
A difficult decision is upon you:
Keep the prize you so much desire,
Or the newfound friends that accompany you.
The choice is yours to make and yours alone."

Azure knew what she had to do. She decided. The emerald door in front of her was now open. She ran through it and climbed the steps. She found herself outside. She was now free.

This tale ends with Azure. Her search is now complete. She has achieved her goal. Azure looks at the horizon, while taking in the Dream Flower's scent. She looks at the horizon without looking back, she didn't look back, back at the smoke that rose from a nearby place, a place she was not long ago.

Part Two
The Tale of the Forgotten Witch

Chapter One

The Forbidden Forest

This story is about me, I call myself Globalea. I don't quite remember much about me, I remember neither my name, nor my childhood. What I remember is something that no one else will forget. The battle I lost to evil.

You see, I was a ruler of a forest, the forest that I named Grandea. The forest was sacred to all lands, yes, sacred and mysterious. There were flowers in that forest that contained hidden powers, powers that would clad the holder with extra abilities to their own. In that forest, there were also many kinds of beasts, all of them dangerous, and more importantly, powerful.

I also ruled the mountain whose large feet were the foothold of the sacred forest. The mountain I called White Mist, for the mountain was always clad in a beautiful white haze. And in that haze many beasts could be found, powerful beasts, beasts that no human could ever defeat, let alone tame.

How did I rule? Well, that question must be twirling in your mind right now. The thing is, I'm not quite human. Well, I am a human, or at least I started out as one, but along the way, I became something else... I became a witch. I am a powerful sorceress. I don't know if I became one out of latent talent, or just hard work, but I am one nonetheless.

I found myself in the sacred forest when I was young. I didn't know where I belonged, or where was my family, nor if I even had a family, so I chose to stay in the forest and make it my home.

The forest itself wasn't that dangerous, the beasts living in it were making it like that. But soon after my arrival, I had made the forest my home. I was able to escape the most dangerous beasts with ease, and I tamed most of the smaller beasts by submitting them to my will.

There was a village near the forest, we were like neighbours. However, no one from that village ever strolled inside the forest. They were mortally afraid of it. Well, they had a good reason for that. Every time one entered the forest, that one was devoured by a beast. Their purpose of entering the forest was unclear to me.

Not long after my arrival, I began working on my magic. I got stronger quite fast; in fact, I manage to become the strongest being in the forest. I submitted all beasts to my will, even the strong ones, the ones that I couldn't do before. Everything in the forest was mine.

The villagers were ignoring my very existence from the moment I arrived. And that angered me. I wanted friends, but I had none. I was afraid to show myself to them. I know what you'll say… you'll say that there was no need for me to fear…but there was!

You see, the first time a villager entered the forest he was chased by a wild boar, a really big wild boar. I helped him escape; I did it by inviting him to my hiding place. I gave him to eat some of my herbs, and gave him some water to drink.

At the beginning, he was somewhat grateful, always looking out if another wild beast was anywhere near my hiding place, not paying any attention to me. However, the very moment his lying eyes fell upon me, a look of disgust was formed on his face. He shunned me! He shunned me, even though I had just saved his life. And he did it because the clothes I was wearing were torn and dirty, and my hair wasn't straight and clean. He shunned me.

I got angry. Very angry. He saw my anger grow and he stammered. He saw my anger grow into fury, and he smiled nervously asking me to forgive his manners. But I wasn't listening to his deceits. I knew he was lying. The only thing he wanted was to be saved, no matter the cost. And that angered me even more. I screamed.

The moment I screamed the forest shivered, and I ran away from him. I heard him asking me to help him, but I ignored him, I just ran. He tried following me, but I knew the forest quite well, and I was also much smaller than him, and because of that, I was able to hide to places that he could never do.

I hid. He lost me. I saw his eyes. In his eyes, I saw fear and anger. I felt joy. *He shunned me, and now he's going to pay for it,* I thought. I turned away and lied down. I heard him screaming, badmouthing me. Then he ran again, but he did not go far. I heard him scream again, desperately. And then there was silence.

After that incident, I never bothered helping the other people who got themselves lost in the forest. I knew it wasn't worth it. I knew that if I were to risk my life for them, nothing good would come out of it or at least nothing good for me. In the end, I would get the same look as I did the first time.

But that incident hardened me. I felt furious for the first time. And even though it scared me, I must admit that it also made me feel great. I had found joy in being angry at the villagers, it gave me strength. In a way, it motivated me to become powerful.

The fact is, however, that regardless of my experience with that foul man, the villagers were unaware of me, and I had to do something to change that. Ha! And I did the one thing that would please me most. I declared myself their ruler.

There were, of course, some that thought they could resist. They entered the forest to slay me. But as you probably can imagine, they never reached me. My beasts tore them apart. Well, not all of them. I allowed one to escape only to warn the other villagers of what doom they can expect if they don't submit to me willingly.

The man cried out what he saw. Most of them were convinced that it was best to surrender, but there was a man that thought otherwise. He climbed to the highest point of the village and began his beautiful speech...something about a gift that what given to them not long ago, and something about them protecting that gift with their lives if they must, for that gift was the greatest gift of all.

He didn't say much, for I got bored and used my magic on him and turned him into stone. And because of that trick, they assumed that I control the earth. But also, thanks to that trick they submitted themselves to me. And because they did it quickly, without much resistance, I honoured their two requests. The first one was to allow them to continue their lives as they were, without me interfering in their daily lives; and the second one was to give permission, to some of them, to go and built a town near the village.

Yes, I was quite generous, I know. Of course, they had to pay tribute to stay alive, for even my generosity has its limits. If one didn't manage to pay, that one would die.

But the most important law I placed on them was the law that forbade them in entering my forest. No one was allowed to enter it, unless of course, one had my permission. The only certainty is that no one could escape after trespassing.

Chapter Two

The White Mist Mountain

The mountain I called White Mist was pretty easy to conquer, but harder than the village. The mountain I had to conquer myself. I had to go all the way up there to make sure all the beasts were my followers.

The good thing is that I didn't climb up, I flew. Well, I didn't actually fly; I mounted a big hawk, with broad wings, and flew up. When I arrived to the mountain I was amazed, for the view was beautiful, like nothing I had ever seen.

It was the first time I had ever been to the mountain in person. My mind was often up there, enslaving beasts to my will, but in body I hadn't had the pleasure of going there sooner.

When I arrived, some of my slaves were waiting for me. There were some cute creatures with really big teeth, yes, very cute indeed. I bid them to guide me towards the ruler of the mountain.

Chapter Three

Showdown in the Dark

I walked the paths of the mountain, following my slaves, in search of the ruler of the mountain, knowing exactly what I had to do. The paths were narrow; one wrong step could result in a disaster.

My slaves were fully devoted to me. They even swayed their friends that I hadn't enslaved yet. And as I walked, more and more creatures were submitting to my will.

There were, of course, some beasts that didn't want to listen to reason and they attacked me. How did I handle them? Simple. I had to use *my* power of *persuasion*. I raised my hand, and pointed at those winged-beasts. Then, the next moments they burned, one after the other. After this, all the winged creatures nearby were enslaved.

The mist of the mountain was getting thicker and thicker as I climbed. It was weird. The more I climbed, the more I felt like someone had his gaze fixed on me. How could that someone see me in that mist...?

I had no reason to fear anything. I knew I was more powerful than everyone. No one could defeat me. All creatures that dared defy me were obliterated to the point of absolute nothingness.

My slaves led me to a secret pathway through a crevice on the mountain side. The pathway was kind of narrow for me, but for my slaves was perfect. I was displeased at first for leading me in that pathway, but that soon changed. It changed after I saw as to where that pathway led.

It led me into another corridor, a much wider one, than the one that I had just been through. The unfortunate fact of that corridor was that it wasn't lighted by anything, so I lighted one of my candles, compliments of my village.

When the fragile fire lit the corridor, a warm pleasing feeling was also lighted in my heart. The walls of this corridor were masked by a curtain of diamonds, rubies, sapphires and emeralds. And all of it was mine.

I sensed movements inside the walls, but I didn't care, for I knew that they couldn't hurt me. So I walked. I walked to find out where that corridor would lead me to.

It led me to a doorway. It was shut. It wouldn't budge, not even to my powers. But the doorway reacted to my powers. Letters were shown with a white radiance; the letters then scrambled and formed a riddle. The riddle went like this:

"What is that which cries at night? To fright its prey, and suck its might,

What is that which cries at night? With eyes shining blue, and howl of white,

If you want to proceed, you must answer both."

The truth is that I didn't really expect such a riddle. It was quite easy. I answered almost immediately. The answers were Bat and Wolf. And I was careful to answer in the correct manner. You see, I had to give the answers the same way the questions were given. And that was the tricky part, for if I were to give my answer the other way around, something really bad would've happened to me.

The doorway opened after I gave the correct answer, but that wasn't the only change. A pouch that was loaded with something, materialized in front of me. I took it without opening it.

Then I walked through the doorway, but this time I led the way, and not my slaves, for my powers were guiding me, and I didn't trust those beasts; in fact, I didn't trust anyone.

I walked and walked for quite a while. I, once again, walked through narrow pathways and steps, however, this time it was inside the mountain and not around it.

I lighted plenty of candles, and I had them floating near me to illuminate my path. Yes, it's quite handy to have magic, for if I didn't have it, I couldn't light up my candles, let alone make them to stay afloat.

There came a time that I reached a dead-end. Well, to be more precise, I reached another door, and this one was shut as well.

However, the good news with this one was that it opened forcefully. I smashed it with my powers.

I walked through the door and found myself in a wide space. I didn't expect this, to be honest. There were pillars that seemed handmade, but that was impossible, for the legend says that no mortal had ever managed to even climb the mountain, let alone enter into its deeper caverns, and built pillars and statues.

But that wasn't the only one surprise that I faced. The other incredible sight I saw was the beast that lived inside this chamber. It was a very large beast, a white wolf with wings; the wings, however, was that of a bat, and its teeth also. My guess was that it was the ruler of the mountain.

Well, at any rate, it was, do or die, for the moment I stepped in, the beast woke up. And it had a pretty hungry look on its face. Not that I cared, but it must've been quite hungry; but the one thing it didn't know was that I wasn't on the menu.

It flapped its ugly wings and flew. It howled and made a strange move. It looked to me that it was ready to create a gust to put out the candles. And that would've been bad, for I might've been able to prevent them not to actually melt, but if a gust was to hit them, I wouldn't be able to do anything to prevent them from going out.

I was right about the beast's motives. It caused quite a massive gust; I figured its way of thinking right away. Wolves and bats have excellent senses, and since that beast had both traits, it would have the advantage in the darkness.

However, I didn't let it get away with it. Since I anticipated that attack, I managed to figure out a way to somehow preserve my flames. And I did it so by eating them. Well, to be more precise, I inhaled them. But that, of course, had the same result that the gust attack would have had.

But thanks to my quick thinking, I wasn't afraid. I felt that I had the upper hand in this fight. Well, to be honest, I was the only one that thought that. The wolf had another opinion. It growled hungrily and landed on the ground softly.

I had no sight, for there was no light, but I was able to sense the savage beast. I was not at all scared of it, for I knew that I could slay it. The only problem with that was the fact that none of my attacks was landing. The creature was really fast; after all, the darkness was its natural habitat.

It attacked me plenty of times, but I somehow dodged each and every one of its attacks, for thanks to my powers I was able to sense them coming; but dodging its attacks was getting me nowhere, and it did it fast. I had to land a successful strike; however, the darkness was pitched, and I felt like it was growing in strength, and that could only mean that the creature itself was getting more powerful also.

It was obvious to me as to why that creature was the ruler of the mountain, and why no other creature had ever managed to defeat it. However, I wasn't like the lame beasts that inhabited that mountain, I was clever and extremely powerful.

From the moment I figured out the situation, I brainstormed for a way to alter it and make it favour me. And I was successful in finding a way! I had already prepared for it from the beginning of the battle. The fire I inhaled!

So I began working on a plan as to how I'll use my fiery powers. I had to use them properly, for if I didn't, I would've found myself in a really tough bind, since the fire-type powers weren't really mine. If I didn't use them in the correct way, they would run out and that would be disastrous.

The difficult part, however, wasn't the manner I would choose to attack it with, but rather the time I had left to do so, for I sensed that the more the seconds were passing, the more the darkness's power was increasing. And that was quite bad.

I began unfolding my strategy right away. My first concern was to make sure that the creature was pinned down to the ground, for an airborne enemy was more difficult to oppose. I smacked my palms to the ground and chanted a spell of my own creation:

"Bind the sky with your mighty vines, and grand me control of their great desires, to make them regret their every decision,
To make them fear my very existence."

HA! With that spell, fiery vines took over the ceiling, making it impossible for anything to fly. I forced the creature to land. Of course, it didn't have much of a choice, for if it was unfortunate enough to get caught to the vines, and not only it was burned, but it also received additional damage from all the thorns that grew on them…the truth is when I invented the spell, the vines were normal, but as my power grew, I was able to mix it up a bit.

Now there was some light in the chamber. But even with that faint light, the battle was still in the darkness, and even though the darkness's power stopped growing, the battle was more critical than ever. The creature's power stopped increasing because of me, and that angered it. The darkness wasn't pitched as it was before, but it was still heavy.

It attacked me relentlessly. I, however, did not fret. I knew I could handle it. I stripped a vine and whipped it. It growled, it growled like a mad dog, filled with rage and despair, for my attack had an effect, and a good one at that. Thanks to the added effect of fire, the extent of the damage that one strike caused was great.

As the battle raged on, the creature was getting closer and closer into striking me. That, of course, would be disastrous for me, since its nails and fangs were extremely sharp, and its body strength was probably unreal. But, that was OK, for I enjoyed the fact that it was gaining ground in our battle. That way, I could learn more and more about myself, and of the world.

I was, somehow, able to match my speed with its speed, no matter how crazy it sounds. The only problem was this: in order for me to make sure there was at least a little light in the chamber, I had to use the fire that I had inhaled. I used it to make sure that the vines were always burning. There were times when sparks were exploded from the thorns, and they were quite dangerous, but I'll get to that later.

I knew that my time was limited, so regardless of how much I enjoyed it, I had to finish the battle before it was too late. So I acted quickly. I unsealed some of my powers that I held back, not that I held them back for concern or anything, I held them back for the sake of amusement, you know, it was more amusing to toy with your victim. But now there was no time to have fun, besides I already had it.

By releasing my hidden powers, I gained the upper hand right away. I whipped the creature again and again, with great pleasure I might add, and then I tried getting close to it, that way, I would be able to test on it some of my spells.

And I did. I closed in on it, and I waved my hand slowly thrice. After I did it, it was like time got frozen for a few seconds, and then an explosion took place upon the creature, and the creature was badly hurt. Now, you must wonder as to why the creature just sat there quietly and allowed me to cast my spell…right? Well, the answer is simple, the creature couldn't move, for I trapped it with my whip.

Then to humiliate, even more, I threw it to the vines that covered the ceiling. It got a great deal of damage from there too. Unfortunately, my last move had a quite unsettling result…the fire that was infused with the vines burned out. Only one vine from the ceiling and the vine I already held were still burning.

Thanks to my last move, the light in the chamber was almost diminished. Thanks to my last move, I almost lost the battle, for the creature was still alive and well, well…not quite well…but you get the picture, I almost lost because I went too far.

But the good news is that I didn't lose, for there were two vines still burning, and that light was more than enough for me to win. After all, the creature wasn't the only being in that chamber that was furious. For some reason, I was furious also.

My desire to kill the beast was long gone. What I wanted to do to it was far more humiliating. I wanted to hurt more than its body. I wanted to hurt its pride. I wanted to make it suffer to the point of oblivion. I would make it my most dedicated slave.

With the two whips at hand, I was ready for anything. The creature seemed ready for everything also. But I wasn't afraid. I knew I would win. Regardless of the situation, regardless of the difficulty, regardless of the enemy, I would win.

Our clash was terrible. My whips were sparking as they were landing hits. The creature was struggling to land a hit, of course, with no luck. I dodged each and every attack, some, of course, I intercepted; I did it either with my powers or my whips.

This showdown in the dark went on for longer than I had imagined. Surprisingly, the creature had more stamina that I gave it credit for. Its futile resistance, however, did not last for long. I showed the creature what true greatness means, I showed it what true power means.

It didn't take long for it to fall. It didn't take long for it to see its destiny. It didn't take long for it to see its true purpose for existing.

The creature realized that what it was doing was wrong. It realized that fighting me for supremacy was wrong, for there was never a question as for who was superior. I was superior from the very beginning.

The creature submitted to my will, and I named it White Fang. And White Fang was my most horrible and loyal slave. It served me well. It was guarding my domain, up there in the mountain. And as a reward for its great service, I made sure to feed it with those who didn't pay tribute. After all, I am a compassionate person.

After this little skirmish, I descended down to my forest, in thoughts of what my next moves would be.

Chapter Four

The Ethereal Flowers

As I already mentioned before, in my forest, there was a rich variety of flowers; and all of them had a unique ability stored within them. That ability was given to the holder. As you might expect, however, there were side-effects, when one was blessed with the unique gift of a flower. Think of it like cost, or consequence.

The powers these flowers give are mysterious. At first, everyone thought that the powers were given accordingly to each individual's personality traits. But of course, that was lame and totally untrue. One's personality had nothing to do, with the power one would gain from the flower. The truth is simpler, and at the same time, more complicated than that.

You see, each flower has a unique ability stored within it. The blessing of each flower differs with each other; some differ much, others differ a little. But the important thing is, that no matter how similar are two flowers, they're not the same, and so are their powers.

Now, as the flowers differ with each other, so does the price for using one. If the ability of the flower is weak, then so is the price for using it. However, if the ability of the flower is stronger, then so is the price. That is the basic principle of the ability flowers, or else known as 'Ethereal Flowers'.

The Ethereal Flowers could be found everywhere in the world. There were places, of course, that didn't have many of them; and there were others that could even have only one. But, usually, at the places where a great number of flowers was to be found, those flowers were common flowers, granting the basic abilities that one could hardly even notice. Those abilities were mainly about brute strength, and a little sharper intuition.

The places that had fewer flowers were more difficult to acquire them, and naturally the abilities they granted were sharper than the abilities the common flowers were giving. Some of those flowers were located on mountains, hilltops, ravines and places like that, places that were tough to reach.

The lands that had only one Ethereal Flower were the special lands. In those lands, the flower was unique. It gave the holder an incredible ability, ability that no other even reminded it. It would give the word 'unique' a whole new meaning. But as you probably figured, in order for one to acquire that one Flower, that one had to give up something really precious. And the side effect was mainly the hole in that one's heart for giving up that something precious.

The only places in the world that had all kinds of Flowers were two. The one was a forest I used to live in, the forest that once was known as the Golden Woods, before I renamed it to Grandea. As for the other place, I don't know pretty much anything for it. Neither its name nor its location; the only thing I know about it, is that it's really far away from the Grandea forest.

Chapter Five

My First and Most
Devastating Mistake

The years passed and I had complete domination. I ruled the whole area. The mountain's beasts were completely loyal to me and they would devour any and all life forms that spoke against me.

The villagers had sent a party of sturdy men to a field near their village and began building their town. They did it so with my consent, but that didn't alter the fact that the people that inhabited the town would also have to pay tributes for their lives.

The town was built slowly, but they managed to make it perfectly with the first try. They didn't have to repair or redo anything in their town. The truth is that I don't know how they did it. I was under the impression that they were uneducated, you know, total peasants.

But they, somehow, managed to construct the town with an exceptional delicacy, and that delicacy implied that they did have some sort of education. Nevertheless, I couldn't comprehend it back then, for that kind of education was advanced, too advanced for the likes of them to possess.

I kept wondering as to where they could've got this kind of education. Who taught them and why. You know stuff like that. But I could not find an answer. Hell, I couldn't even guess! Their knowledge of some things outgrew even mine. And the bad thing was that I couldn't do anything to stop them.

Well, not that I didn't try, but you know, when I did try it was already too late. Let me explain. I suppose that you do remember when I told you about my promise to them, my promise that I would not interfere with their daily lives and all, right?

Right! And the truth is that I didn't interfere with it. Until, of course, they had shown that defiant attitude, by building their town with incredible efficiency and speed. When they showed the first signs of defiance, I had no choice but to keep a more watchful eye over them.

What I did was simple. I had some of my minions of the forest live among them, you know, to keep them safe from any invader. And I also had some of my winged minions watch over the town and the village, and with their sharp eyesight, I was able to see much.

But the peasants were able to hide well their rebellion; I couldn't find the evidence that would prove it. Even when some of my darling carnivore beasts, that I send to guard the peasants, got a little hungry and ate four of them, they didn't do anything, they just moved on.

There came a time when I heard a whisper about a book that contained their history! Yes, I knew that if that whisper was a true one, I would've been able to know everything there is to know about them. For instance, I would've learned what kind of great scheme they were planning to overthrow me, and most importantly, I would learn who infused in them the wisdom they possessed.

All I needed to learn was if that whisper had any truth in it. Sounds simple, huh? Well, it sure sounds simple, but it was neither simple nor easy, for no one would ever admit its existence. Yes, I had met a dead-end. I threatened I tortured, I slayed, but no luck. No one, and when I say no one, I mean no one, yes, no one said anything about it, they only kept saying that it doesn't exist.

But I, Globalea, did not give up on that search; I only pretended that I did, so that I can fool those peasants. And as you might expect, they bought it. They had actually believed that I gave up on the search. How did I make them believe it, you ask? Well, it's quite simple! I just ordered my minions to return to the forest. That way, none of my minions had their watchful eye on them from the ground or the air.

They felt relieved from that move, I'm sure. However, they did not count on my powers. They foolishly thought that I could not see them when they were doing a mischief... they sure were naive! But, I'm not complaining about it, for thanks to that, I was able to find out that their so-called Book of History does exist.

Yes, it existed! I found out about it completely out of luck... Yes, yes, yes, it was a total coincidence, me finding out about it. Surprisingly, the book wasn't hidden in the town, as I had suspected, but in the village, where most of the elders had decided to stay. And ironically, the village was the place that I had stationed less of my minions too. Oh well...

The important thing, and mostly in my mind at that time, was the fact that I had finally discovered that the book existed, and I also had its location. Well, I didn't know its exact location, but at least I knew where to look.

Unfortunately, for the first time in my days as the Queen, luck was against me. When I was finally able to find the exact location of the book, I got restless and eager, and way to hasty. I did not wait, I could not wait. My hatred got the best of me, and I personally assaulted the village. I burned the hut that my powers guided me that it was it that held the book, and I personally searched it as it was on fire.

It wasn't there. My powers could not be fooled. It should've been there. But it wasn't. And that angered me, it really angered me. There was a couple that lived in that hut. And I asked nicely where my book was. They said that they didn't read. That response angered me, of course. Then I asked them again the same question, only to get the same answer.

But then it hit me. I could never get the truth that way. An ingenious plan came into mind, and I put it to work right away. I told them that if my memory served me, they had a son. Then I asked them where he was. The woman, which was probably the mother, had an outburst of fake tears, and the father pretended to be crushed by my question. Quite the bad acting they demonstrated, I must say. Then they said that their son had a tragic accident the other day and died. I was certain that they lied, and it was confirmed by my powers, so I slayed them as they stood, for lying and trying to cheat me, their Queen!

Sadly, I could not sense that anyone knew the whereabouts of the boy, who probably had the book with him, so I burned a few more huts to punish them, and then I returned to my forest, completely enraged by my failure. I sat at my wooden throne, that I myself had crafted, and began brainstorming as to how I'll find that accursed book.

I didn't sleep that night. I could only think. I thought of pretty much every little detail of the area nearby, and concluded that the child shouldn't be far. Well, the truth is that it had limited options to choose from! It couldn't return to the village, for if it did, I would sense its life force, since it had similar with its parents, which I already slayed. It couldn't go to the city, for nothing would stop me to incinerate it completely. It couldn't stay abroad on the fields, for my watchers were everywhere, both on the ground and in the sky. It could never get to the mountain. So the only option it had was to enter my forest in an attempt to somehow fool me, by getting entangled into the webs of its 'enemy'.

As I concluded to that, I suddenly sensed that someone intruded my forest, and I knew that someone was none other the child, which held my book. I moved quickly, I ordered my beasts to close off all exits of the forest, and I headed towards the place I sensed the intruder.

But as I glided towards that place, something happened, something that I could never had anticipated. The life force I was sensing disappeared completely, leaving no trace behind. And the disturbing thing was that it happened suddenly, with no reason, for none of my servants was anywhere near it.

So my only guess is that it was the work of an Ethereal Flower. But I never knew an Ethereal Flower that could do that, and that confused me, for I wasn't certain that it was the work of a flower for sure, it could be that the child had powers of its own, and if it could conceal itself, it could possibly do much more.

I reached the point that I last sensed the intruder. It was a wide-open space, really beautiful, with no trees and many flowers, flowers of many kinds. That wide- open space was surrounded by bushes. Hah, if I only knew then…

I stood in the middle of it like a statue. I was rooted in that place for many hours, but nothing happened. I sensed nothing. The good thing was that regardless of what kind of ability that little brat had, it would be meaningless against the barrier I had placed around my forest.

The barrier did not keep people out, only other sorcerers, wizards, magicians, warlocks and anyone else who dealt with magic. The normal people could come and go as they pleased, the only thing it did for them was to warn me that someone entered or left my forest. The only exceptions would be those who held a unique Ethereal Flower, and sadly I couldn't do anything about that small detail, for I wasn't strong enough to overpower the strongest of the Ethereal Flowers.

After many, many hours, when the sun was lost, and the full moon took its place, I returned, and I sat on my throne. I fell asleep right away, even though I didn't plan it. How foolish I was not to stay awake, for if I had, things would probably be different now.

I felt a sudden a strong shiver. I did not shiver, the forest did. I don't really know if it was my spell that did it, or if it was the so-called Heart of the Forest the peasants kept mumbling about, but I sensed that someone escaped from my clutches.

I glided to the end of the forest as fast as I could, but when I did, I found nothing. The brat was long gone. And I could still sense nothing, nor did my beasts see anything of it. I was in a complete darkness of its whereabouts after that moment for many years.

So, I, once again, returned to my throne, defeated. My first mistake that was, the mistake I paid dearly, a mistake that cost me everything.

Chapter Six

Premonition

I don't know what it meant, and to be honest, I still don't know what it means. But I will, nevertheless, tell you about it. About the premonition, I had in the night after the child escaped from me.

After the child had escaped from me, I returned to my throne, defeated. I could not sleep. Frustration kept me awake. My inner anger boiled because of my failure. And my unanswered questions were tormenting me; they tormented me in a very large scale. Because of all that negativity, a strong insomnia was over me.

The thing is that the negative feelings were empowered, not only by the failure itself but also from the fact that it was my very first failure. And my insomnia was upon me for days because of that. I could not sleep, not at all. I could not get over my failure, no matter how much I tried.

After many days of sleepless nights, and restless mornings, finally sleep took me. Yes, I fell into a deep slumber. Too deep perhaps, for when I fell into it, I could not escape it. No matter how much I tried, I was tied up onto something strong, something that prevented me to wake up.

As you probably can imagine, however, I did manage to escape from my dream. I say dream, cause that is what I thought of it then, how naive I was…you see, I did not want to admit that I could not explain the premonition that I had, so I closed off the subject in my mind, by simply saying that it was a mere dream.

If I were mature enough to admit that it was more than a dream, regardless if I had the knowledge to explain it or not, maybe things wouldn't have turned out as they had. Oh well… Back then, I remembered only fragments about my premonition, mostly images. But now I remember it whole. Pay attention!

When I fell asleep, I felt like I glided towards a dark castle. The castle was massive, and it had many defence mechanisms, mechanisms that would eradicate any and all enemies who were foolish enough to assault it. However, the guards that were stationed there did not react to my presence, and that's probably, cause I wasn't really there, only my spectral form was there, not my material form.

I got the feeling that the castle I had just visited was really far away from my forest. I sensed a vibe of great evil. It was like the castle itself wanted to devour me. Even the guards looked evil, with their shiny swords and armour, and their clean faces.

Despite all the evil, I moved forward. I never stopped gliding. And the good thing about being a spectral body is that one can go through walls and such, and that is what I did. I passed through the gates and witnessed in disgust the most repulsive sight. Everything in the courtyard was hideous. The only thing that I liked about it was that it had many, many flowers. Unfortunately, I couldn't tell if they were Ethereal Flowers, or regular ones.

As I advanced deeper and deeper into the castle, my disgust grew. I saw fountains and statues, and monuments... Humph, I won't continue with this.

I moved forward to the point I reached the royal palace guards. They were guarding the gate, the main gate, which most likely behind it was the Lord of the castle. Yes, yes, yes. They probably protected their lord...HA!

I went passed the gate and entered casually into the main hall of the palace. Immediately I felt uneasy, yes, even scared. Fear, I felt. It was unsettling indeed, for I hadn't had that emotion for many a year. Yes...

However, regardless of me being afraid, I kept on going forward. I really wanted to see with my own two eyes the ruler of this castle. Yes, my desire was stronger than my fear. And the truth is that I don't know if that was good or bad. For better or worse, I moved forward instead of turning back.

I glided forward and saw more disgusting artefacts. I won't even mention them. It took me long to reach the end of the hallway, and finally enter the main chamber, where the king resided.

I saw many powerful items in there, most of them I did not understand at all; but I could, no doubt, sense their awesome strength. The king was sitting on his throne, and he was resting. HA! What kind of a ruler would take a nap casually, like this, on his throne? Ridiculous!

The thing is that I sensed a great deal of power from him. He was. As I said, casually napping, and yet his power was higher than mine…and that, as you can imagine, caused my fear to grow, rapidly.

I was wrapped in fear. I could not think. I could not see anything but him. I was terrified to even attempt removing my eyes off of him. He seemed really kingly, the way he was dressed, the way he was fast asleep, everything. I was both afraid of him, and mesmerized by his stature.

However, at that point, I had forgotten that I was in his realm in a mere spectral form. I had forgotten that in his realm there were his rules. I had forgotten that I was vulnerable. I had forgotten that he was more powerful than anything I had felt before.

This premonition ended badly, as you probably can imagine. I remember clearly what happened. The terror I felt from that person. I remember him, opening his eyes slowly as if he was suddenly aware of my presence, and then his face hardened, making him look terrible. I think I also heard him say something like, "I know what you are, and you have no place here."

Yes, after that, everything took the worst course possible. I remember that suddenly everything around me disappeared, and that man was standing face to face with me. And I felt like he was always there watching me, as if he was never asleep, peacefully, on his throne.

Everything went dark, and then I sort of woken up in a dungeon.

I say sort of, because I couldn't tell if I was awake or asleep. All I know was that I was completely tied up with chuckles and chains. Chains that were so heavy, that even my very mind could not think; I couldn't even move, let alone try escaping.

I felt heavy and extremely weak, like something had taken away not only my magical powers, but my very energy of my existence. I felt that the darkness was taking me, little by little, slowly, but steadily. I was afraid, very, very afraid. And then...

I woke up.

Chapter Seven
The Intruder

When I woke up from that special dream, cold sweat was running down my forehead. It was like my very existence had received a powerful strike of fear. Of course, back then, I did not admit it. I was in complete denial. I refused to admit that I was afraid from that experience I had. I wanted to convince myself that it was just a bad dream, a nightmare that had no point in thinking about it.

Perhaps, that was the reason for me not remembering much of it. It was probably my own denial that was blinding me, yes, my own denial it was blinding me from the truth. And not just that truth, there were many other truths, that even though they were in front of me at the time, I ignored them.

What I mean when I say other truths, you ask? Well, I'll get to that right away. You see, just a few days after my unpleasant premonition, I had an uninvited guest in my forest. That guest was nothing like the peasants that live in the village and the town; he was different.

Well, let's take it from the top, for I'm getting ahead of myself. A few days had passed after my premonition, and I was, as I told you, in complete denial, trying to convince myself that it was just a bad dream. My arrogance and pride were at their zenith back then. I could only see myself and no one else.

And then, out of nowhere, the barrier I had placed around the forest for protection against other humans with magical powers was activated. I sensed that it send someone flying. The force, of course, of that impact was great, but I sensed that the one, who got blasted away, got up immediately after his fall. And that was quite bad, for that impact was supposed to knock out anyone and everyone who was foolish enough to try crossing my borders.

The intruder did not give up, and between us, why should he? He analysed the barrier in just a few minutes, and then he unleashed a powerful ice attack. As you can probably imagine my barrier was pierced to smithereens, and the intruder advanced like nothing happened.

Chapter Eight

A Petal Dance of Fire and Ice

The scam that invaded my domain I can never forget. He was handsome, yes, but that is not the reason that I'll never forget him; our battle was glorious! Pfft, once again I'm getting ahead of myself. Here we go...

The intruder shattered my barrier into a million pieces with a single spell, and then he casually strolled in my forest, you know, like he was having a pleasant walk or something. Well, it's not that I blame him for it, for my forest was one of the most beautiful places in the world, so it would be strange if he didn't enjoy walking in it.

The strange part was that he seemed to somehow know the forest and its secrets. He seemed familiar with the Ethereal Flowers. He was whispering to them, and that is something only a few do in the whole world. Very few knew that the Ethereal Flowers were like living beings and that they would serve one better if they get attached to that one; of course, if they get too attached, the same thing would happen with the person having it, meaning that it would be close to impossible to abandon it.

Yes, the intruder seemed to know about that. And that seemed really strange to me, him knowing about it. Very,

very few knew about the Ethereal Flowers, let alone their habits and everything.

There was something else that surprised me. The intruder was also talking to the trees and the ground. Yes, that was odd. I could not figure out his motives. Why would he speak to something that could not be proved useful to him in any way? And besides that, the trees and the ground did not have a will; they were bound to stay in the same place as long as they existed.

The intruder knew my location, but he didn't approach me right away. First, he encircled the entrance of the forest, as he was seeking something, and then he began moving forward, towards me, with the same encircling method. However, he moved slowly. And that was, yet another, sign that he was actually seeking something. Quite fearful the intruder, huh…?

HA! Don't tell me that you already forgot of my state? The state I was at the time…well, let me remind you…I was wild! I figured that he was up to something right away and even began brainstorming of possible artefacts that he could be searching for.

The first and obvious guess was, of course, an Ethereal Flower. But that theory did not hold for long, for he bypassed pretty much every flower that could be proved in any way useful; useful to combat and witchcraft. So my next theory was of something that it just couldn't be! But it made perfect sense! In that absurd situation, that absurd guess was the best I had. He was seeking the History Book!

Why would he, ever, search for that book? That was my first question. How did he even know of its existence? What was it, really? Could it hold more answers that the ones

I was searching for? What was it that he searched for? Who the hell was he?

Many questions I had, but I could find no answer for them. At least, not while having that passive stance. But something was making me hesitate in attacking him. I don't know what, maybe it was just a gut feeling, or maybe a higher kind of power was guiding me not to begin the battle.

At any rate, I waited. I waited until he came to me. I knew he would. Yes, there was no doubt in my mind that he would confront me. After all, he had no other choice, for if he had failed, which he did, in finding what he was searching for, he would have no other choice but to try and asking me about it.

Of course, that's not all. The artefact that he was searching for could very well be, on the other side of my forest, meaning right behind me. So the only way he could get there was through me…Humph, like that was ever going to happen…

I waited patiently. I made myself comfortable on my throne, and I waited for his arrival. As I had anticipated, that took long…he searched quite well, I dare say, but of course, with no luck. He found nothing.

I felt restless. I knew he was approaching me, and that made me feel uneasy. Of course, back then, I did not admit it to myself, so I just turned it into a rage, just to be certain. But I wasn't angry with myself, or with the intruder. My rage was pointed towards my dream. Yes, towards my premonition, for it was because of that premonition that my confidence was shaken to the point of doubt. Well, to be more exact, I pointed my rage towards the lord of that dark castle I had visited.

Well, at any rate, my doubts were consumed by rage, and once again, I felt powerful. It was a good thing that it happened, of course, for that man wasn't one someone could take on while second-guessing one's self. He was really powerful. But since I wasn't frightened by anything, I had pushed the matter of the dream to a distant corner of my mind, I faced the intruder when he finally arrived, and I only saw him for what he really was: an intruder, a trespasser, someone who I needed to destroy, for he was a threat to my dominion.

Well, he arrived and he faced me. When he did, my rage grew, for he was not at all scared. He faced me like he was facing a peasant. He was dark-haired and quite handsome, with bright blue eyes and a powerful glance. He was tall, maybe even taller than me, and he wore black robes. It was obvious to me that he dealt with dark magic. Then again, so did I.

He introduced himself with high honours. At first, I heard that he called himself 'The Dog Master', and as you can imagine, I repeated it, and I burst into a loud laughter…and even if there was a smidge of anxiety left in me, it was gone after that.

However, he did not find it funny…shocker. He was annoyed, and he introduced himself once again, normally this time. He said that he was 'The Dark Master'. And before he continued, I interrupted him, and said that the name he chose for himself was oh-too-original.

That, of course, angered him, and then he just said that his name was Poseidon. Now, that was a good name, and I, right away, wondered as to why the hell he changed it. Oh well…

I demanded to know his purpose for invading my territory. He laughed at me and said that it wasn't mine. And after that response, my rage, once again, began to boil. But I didn't move. I just asked him, once again, of his purpose in my forest.

He, however, did not give the same answer. He had probably felt the dramatic increase to my magical power-level. He was once again, courteous. He asked me to leave to search the forest to his heart's content, and that if I were to give it to him, he would reward me with great riches, riches I couldn't imagine that they existed.

HA! But I saw through his lies, just like I did with that peasant back then, and I rose from my throne, completely enraged by his nerve. His nerve to come into my own realm and lie to me, trying to deceive me. Yes, that enraged me, it enraged me to the point that when I got up, all the small pillars of light, that were falling down from the small gaps from the trees, were swallowed up by darkness.

I refused his offer and ordered him out of my realm, or he would pay the price for his actions. He, however, even though a bit stammered by the light show, did not really falter. He only smiled, and said, "As you wish."

And with incredible speed, he moved his hands and took a stance as if he was bending a bow to fire an arrow. At first, nothing was there, but in a blink of an eye, a golden bow appeared and a frozen solid, pure magic, arrow was fired.

However...Poseidon wasn't the only one, with great reflexes and powerful magic. I, too, was powerful! I bended the roots of the trees and created a wooden shield empowered by my magic. The arrow did manage to penetrate it, yes, but it didn't pierce through the entire shield, it just managed to penetrate a little.

He was shocked. Yes, for the first time, I felt him waver, somewhat. But, he got over it almost immediately. And he laughed at me. Well, that was pretty pathetic. It was obvious that it was a fake laughter. Oh well…the fact is that after that first display of magical powers one thing was certain…we were about equals. The outcome of our battle was unclear. Well, at least it would be if any one of us was thinking clearly. Both of us were certain that we'd win the battle.

My only problem was that I didn't know what was giving him such a great motivation. He was tireless. We fought to a standstill for quite a while. And for some reason, no matter my attempts to take the fight to a different spot, he refused to do it. He always came up with something in the middle of the battle to make both of us stick to our ground.

At one point, he raised a massive wall of ice from behind him. That way if I wanted to take the fight elsewhere, I would have no other choice but to go backwards, meaning towards the centre of the forest, a place that for some reason even I avoided going to.

But, I wouldn't play his game. The only reason I wanted to change the scenery a bit, was to ensure my throne's survival. So I had no problem in whipping the floor with him to the place we already were. I stopped trying to force him backwards, and I focused on slaying him.

I played with my thorny whips. I saw him 'dancing' in his attempts to dodge my attacks. Of course, he did manage to dodge some, but not all. And my whips were quite dangerous, since they had poisonous thorns. But even though I wasn't certain whether the poison did enter his system or not, there were no signs of him slowing up. You see, the poison normally caused paralysis.

And then it hit me. He must've held an Ethereal Flower that prevented him from getting poisoned. It must've been quite hard for him to find it, for my poison could never be prevented by a low-level Ethereal Flower, so it was probably quite uncommon.

Well, regardless of the poison, the damage was somewhat extensive. And the wound would slow him down, or so I thought. You see, he healed his wounds with his magic, meaning that he had the powers of a healer. That meant trouble for me, because healing magic was incredibly hard to teach, and once one was taught, that one could never forget about it.

I smiled. I had finally found someone on the same level. I had finally found someone worth slaying. He smiled also, probably thinking the same. And then…

We resumed the battle. Both of us had unleashed our attacks with vengeance. He attacked me with his ice attacks, again and again. At first, it was easy for me to dodge, but as he fired in succession, the precision of his attacks skyrocketed. I was able to block quite many, but as you might imagine there was ' one' that I missed. Back then, I thought that it was the most terrible attack that could've hit me; however, now I believe it was the most harmless attack.

You see, he unleashed an iced breath towards the ground, while he had already released a frozen arrow. I intercepted the arrow with my duo-thorny whips, but I couldn't do anything for the other attack. Apparently, I instinctively refused to jump into the air, because that would just be what he wanted: me into the air, helpless.

So my legs were frozen solid, thanks to that attack. He gloated, of course, saying that I'm not worthy to call myself Queen of that forest. I did not say a word for an answer. I just whipped him with both of my whips. It happened at the same time on both his cheeks.

He fell from the tree branch he was standing on, while groaning pitifully. He was smashed onto the ground-floor, which thanks to him it had that extra ice addition. I laughed at him. He got up, with his pretty face finally ruined with the damage it had received, and anger dripping from his eyes.

Then he told me something that I didn't understand. And to be honest, I still don't. He told me that I had some nerve, me who knew nothing of that forest, to call myself its Queen. He told me that I was completely clueless, and I was going to pay for it. He also told me that it was my time to die, to die in complete ignorance.

The truth is that I didn't pay much heed to his words, for I was trying to get out of the mess I was in. I struggled to break free from the ice that held me. But my magical power could do nothing to ice. Only fire or an extremely powerful spell that concerned nature would do anything to it.

When he told me that it was my time to die, he fired an arrow, an ice arrow that was fuelled with incredibly high magical power. Its density was so high that needles were sprouting from it as it sped. *I knew what I had to do again. It worked before, it will work again*, I thought.

Unfortunately, that wasn't the case. My powers couldn't even bunch the roots from underneath me. And in that split second, I thought I was doomed, for if that arrow had managed to make contact with my body, I would've been slayed for certain.

However, I did not die. I manage to stop the arrow. But it came at a price. You see, in order to stop it, I used both my hands. I grasped it, before hitting me, and used almost all of my magical power to do it. But my magical power wasn't the only price I paid. If you recall, the arrow wasn't pointy only on one end, needles had sprang from its entire body, and so both of my hands were skewered, bleeding like crazy. Fortunately, the arrow vanished right away after it had done its damage because it was a magical one.

I was left speechless gazing at my bleeding hands. Then I heard him speak. At that point, however, I did not pay even the slightest attention to his words, I was just gazing my bleeding hands, you see, it was my first time bleeding.

He said quite many interesting things. Things that if I have paid attention to back then, now things would be totally different for me. He said that I'm a fool. He guessed correctly, that I must've been curious as to why he was talking not only to the Ethereal Flowers (yes, he called them by name), but also to the ground and trees. He said that as the Ethereal Flowers held magical powers within them and one could somewhat manipulate, same thing was applying to the trees and ground. For if one doesn't talk sweetly to the one that is about to manipulate, how does one expect it to serve one properly?

That was his final question. But his chatter did not end. He continued and explained as to why the ground and tree roots did not obey me. It wasn't because I wasn't nice to them;

on the contrary, the entire forest loved me, or at least the part that he explored. So, in order for him to block their assistance towards me, he had to take drastic measures, even if those measures would end up draining most of his magical powers.

The swine blocked my link with the forest by freezing the ground with his enchanted breath. The breath was enchanted by an Ethereal Flower, that's why it was so powerful. By severing the link between me and the forest, I, could no longer receive its help. And then he unleashed the super-charged arrow, with every intention of slaying me. Yes, that was bad.

But at that point, I could not hear any of this. For better or worse, I was stunned by the sight of blood. He unsheathed a sword, a real sword, and began approaching me. When he was halfway near me, something inside me snapped. The truth is I didn't understand what it was, and I still don't. I heard a voice that said, "Fight!"

And I did. I allowed my rage to take complete control of myself, knowing that if I didn't do it, I wouldn't only lose my supremacy of the forest, but I would also lose my life. What was left of my magical power, I concentrated it in my hands and legs, and then I punched the ice that held me with all my strength.

What happened next surprised both of us. The forest shivered, it shivered like a strong earthquake just shook it. The ice that trapped me was shattered, and my feet were finally free. And then I touched the ground. I was finally determined to show my true powers, my real powers.

When I touched the ground, some roots began climbing up on me. As they did, they began crumbling. They rotted and blown away by the wind. And my wounds were gone, they were healed. For I may not have healing powers as Poseidon did, but I could still heal any injury, so long as I can grow any kind of plants, trees and flowers. Yes, I was a witch that loved to dance. You'll understand shortly what I mean by that.

After my wounds were healed, I bent two trees with my will, and grasped the vines that seemed strongest to my eyes. Then I gazed Poseidon in the eye, he was quite frightened; after all, he almost used up all of his magical power on a plan that was certain to slay me. Poor guy…Can't blame him…

But he got over his fear right away. He smiled. Then he showed me something. It was an Ethereal Flower. And that one was extremely rare. It was called the Wild Red Rose, and it gave the holder a fire-type attribute to attack with; and it was located to a land far away, and what's more, it was the only land that it could be found. That could only mean that Poseidon was a traveller.

Humph, he may have had two elements to attack me with, but I was not at all scared. He wasn't the only one who had Ethereal Flowers in his possession. I did too! But at that point, I deemed that it wasn't the right time for them. So I battled him only with my two whips. At that stage of the battle, I didn't stick to the ground, for if yet another attack like the previous one was to happen, I would've been slayed, no doubt about that. So I took my chances and fought him while gliding.

It didn't go well, though. He was able to overpower me while I fought like that. After all, he must've been a sniper, judging by his weapon of choice. His fire attacks were also fired by his bow. It didn't take long to find myself losing hope for that battle.

However, at a certain point, I saw something that gave me hope. I noticed that the ice that covered the ground was much thinner than the time it was cast. And then it hit me! I figured that in order for that ice to exist at all, he had to consume his magical power; and since he was using it to slay me with his bow, or better yet to force me into stepping onto the ground, he couldn't afford to waste his magical power on it.

In order for me to make sure that my theory was correct, I had to glide for as long as possible and to be on the safe side, I glided as high as I could. And after some time, I had the answer. I was right! The ice little by little was melting, to the point that only a little of it was left. I figured that so long as that small part of the ice remained, he could cast once again that spell. But in order for me to check that my theory was correct, I had to land on the ground. And I did…

And, once again, my theory was correct. The small part of ice began growing at a massive speed. And it came towards me, ready to devour me and it did. Or so Poseidon thought, judging from his mocking laughter…

However, he was mistaken! Since I had anticipated such a course, I was able to counter it. When I landed, I immediately smacked my palms onto the ground, and commanded my forest to guard me. When I did, and before the ice devoured me, giant roots encircled me, protecting me from it.

And then, it was my turn to attack. I manipulated the roots that had just shielded me from the ice to smash it. It was really easy, for these roots were from the eldest and sturdiest trees of the forest. Then I ordered them to return into the ground.

I saw Poseidon looking at me, speechless. And he was finally mortally afraid. He was mine. I asked him if he liked dancing. He didn't answer. I asked him if his stunned silence meant a negative answer; still nothing. Then I laughed and told him that I adored dancing. And that he should feel honoured that I would finish our battle that way, he should feel proud because he would be blessed with the privilege to see me dance.

And now it was the time. It was time for me to use my Ethereal Flowers. I held a crystal-blue flower and a red flower, both of them from this forest, both of them quite rare. I may not know their names, but I certainly know the powers they had stored within them, the power of ice and fire.

I began dancing with them at hand. I began dancing an elegant dance, a dance that only royalty would know; I myself did not know how I knew it. And then I infused what was left of my magical power to my flowers, and began the work of my final attack!

Once again, the forest shivered, and Poseidon was still stunned. He snapped out of it; however, the second he realized that he was already inside my attack. He was trapped in a maelstrom of flower petals, petals that were wrapped in flames and in ice.

A beautiful show indeed, I never stopped dancing. I was really beautiful, despite my injuries. Poseidon received many blows from my attack. However, something happened that I didn't expect. Out of nowhere, Poseidon disappeared; probably a flower that gave the ability of teleportation, or maybe he knew how to teleport himself. Who knows? The important facts were two: First fact was that my prey escaped and second, and most important, fact was the fact that I won the battle.

Chapter Nine

The Return of My Mistake

Poseidon escaped me, but there was not a doubt as to who was the victor of our battle. I was the undisputed winner. He fled. The last glimpse I had of him was enjoyable. I saw in his eyes fear and despair.

But I'm really curious about his trick of teleportation. If it's an Ethereal Flower, I would like to get it, and if it's a magical ability, I would like to learn it. At any rate, he escaped in a grand way, and I was not able to locate him. Not that I would chase after him, but it would be good to know if he would assault me again.

His escape was not at all dangerous for me. No matter what he did, he could never defeat me, especially if he was to assault me again in my domain. Besides, next time he would make the mistake of assaulting me, I would be much more powerful, for I had, finally, experienced how it was to fight someone on equal ground.

The battle itself raised my level of power dramatically. I experienced how it felt to hurt. I experienced actual fear; well, the fear was in me beforehand. I experienced how it was to plan, to devise methods in achieving victory, hell, in surviving even, and taking the battle to a higher level, for if I didn't, I wouldn't have survived.

Back then, I didn't give any heed at all to Poseidon's words. I didn't care to learn about the secrets of the forest. I only cared to learn of more spells, of more Ethereal powers, and raise my magical power level. My pride blinded me. My ego got in the way, and because of it, I strayed off my path, the path I had chosen to walk, the path that I have walked ever since I entered the forest as a child. Oh, well... what's done is done... allow me to continue my story...

Many years passed since Poseidon's invasion. As I already told you, I focused all my energy on becoming more powerful. I managed to find many ways of utilizing the Ethereal Flowers; and also, I polished all of my spells, that way I made them stronger and quicker to cast, not to mention more beautiful...

Yes, I had really managed to become strong! But despite all that newfound strength, something was missing. I could sense the void inside me, I could sense it, and I knew that it appeared after my battle with Poseidon. My pride, however, was blinding me from the truth, a truth that I now know oh-too-well, but back then, I was in complete darkness.

As I said, many years passed, since my battle with Poseidon and I felt stronger than ever. I felt like a true Queen. Little did I know that only I was the one who felt like that, for the greatest and most challenging trial I had faced in my life was about to begin.

I made sure that my forest was incredibly well-protected with a three-layered barrier this time, not even a strong wizard would be able to enter easily. Of course, due to my arrogance, I didn't involve the protection of my forest from people with no magical abilities. The massive protection was only for magical beings. The non-magical beings could come and go as they pleased, that did not change; I could still sense them entering, though. So basically, the barrier was pretty much the same as it was; the only changes were that it was three-layered and massively stronger.

And the fateful day came, when my barrier informed me that an intruder just passed through the borders of my forest. However, I could not sense him, not at all. And that could only mean one thing…the intruder was the very same one from back then…back then, when I was searching for the book…back then, when I made my very first mistake… back then, when I allowed the child to escape me, while I had him right there in my forest.

Chapter Ten
Me and Hades, the Finale

I moved quickly. I didn't want to lose time, just like I did before. This time I wanted to capture the brat. So I glided in the moonlight, like a bright yellow star, a yellow star with a grey shadow. And even though I did not know where he was, I somehow knew where he would go.

Yes, he went to the place I had anticipated. The very same place we, somewhat, met the first time he entered my forest. I couldn't clearly sense anything, but I was certain that he was there.

I stood there, in the middle of the very same garden I had stood the last time, and looked at the moon. When I did, I felt more power in me, and thanks to that, probably, I felt something from behind a bush. I asked if he was there, and if he was to come out; and if he did, I wouldn't hurt him. I lied. I had every intention of hurting him; I wanted to make him pay for ridiculing me the first time we met. How wrong I was...

The child came out, he probably believed my words. I saw in his face a look that I had never seen. It really shocked me. Yes, it shocked me to my very core. Even back then it did. I asked him his name. Hades, he answered. "A very nice name indeed," I said.

Then I posed quite many questions, and he answered them all. I asked him if he was the child who had escaped from me the first time, he answered yes. I asked him if he was able to hide from me due to the effects of an Ethereal Flower; of course, he didn't know that the special flowers were called Ethereal, so when I saw that he didn't understand the term, I clarified it, and he, once again, answered yes. Then I asked him about his purpose of entering my forest, if he was in search of an Ethereal Flower; he answered yes. I asked him his reason for wanting it, he answered that he wanted it for a friend. I asked him what for, he answered that his friend was dying and the Ethereal Flower, as I called it, was the only way. My last question was this: I asked him why he was answering me all this, without a second thought or hesitation, why did he answer me with that much sincerity?

He answered, "Because you are the Queen!"

Back then, that angered me. I foolishly thought that he was mocking me. What a fool I was, right? I laughed at him and raised my hand. Roots sprang out and tangled him. He shouted, reminding me of my promise. I ignored him. He then said that no matter what I had done to him, he did not hate me, and that he was actually happy that I won the battle with Poseidon. I didn't believe him. I, once again, foolishly thought that he was lying just to save his skin...just like everybody did in the past.

I commanded the roots to strangle him. But fortunately, something happened when I did that. The forest shivered, and Hades screamed. Then the roots got loosened, and Hades ran away from me. I followed, filled with rage because once again he was making a fool of me.

The truth is I envied Hades. Yes, I envied him. He was handsome, he was smart, and most importantly, he was free. And I...well, I was ugly, hideous even, and no one ever wanted to stay with me, not even my parents; even my sister had forgotten about me. My sister, who I loved more than anything...

I chased Hades. I chased him a long way. He bypassed my throne and entered the territory that even I didn't visit. Yes, he was fearless; and all that just for the sake of a friend. I, of course, back then did not care for any of that. I was consumed by hatred. I wanted to make him suffer, that much of a fool I was.

We reached a point near the centre of the forest. The forest was thicker there, and the trees larger. And for some reason, I was losing track of him all the time. I know the reason now, but I didn't then. I heard him asking for help from the trees. In my heart, I laughed, thinking that it was impossible, for the forest loved me, according to Poseidon at least.

But at a shocking turn of events, the trees actually helped him. They were blocking my way, by sprouting their roots to stop me, and they tried to smash me with their weight. When they did, I did something that probably I regret the most now...I struck the trees that blocked me and burned all the roots that tried to bind me. I did something that I never did before, I hurt the forest.

I saw Hades watch me in distress; even he did not believe that I did that. He ran as fast as he could towards some pink Ethereal Flowers, Flowers that I had never seen in the forest, so I did not know what kind of power they gave. I guessed that it was for his friend. He picked up three. Then, I thought that he would try and make a run for it, I thought that he would try to escape from me.

And he did. With that action, I became certain that the Ethereal Flowers he had picked were for his friend, for if they were meant to be used in a fight with me, he would've used them immediately. How foolish...it's a good thing that due to my rage I couldn't see clearly.

I followed him as he was trying to escape. I attacked him again and again, but with no luck. Strangely enough, every time one of my attacks was close in making contact, they were reverted towards the opposite side. Well, at any rate, he was unharmed, and he sped up in a remarkable way.

We finally reached the place where I resided, and I foolishly thought that the trees would listen to me and do my bidding. But I thought wrong. The forest couldn't forgive me for what I did before. It wouldn't obey me. It didn't recognize me as its ruler anymore.

Of course, back then, instead of realizing this, I attacked the forest again. Hades was urging me to stop. But I couldn't listen. All I could see was my hatred and that blinded me from the truth. I was a true monster.

For some reason, Hades cared, but I couldn't see it. I chased after him relentlessly. He tried to bring me into my senses, but I ignored him. I saw tears in his eyes when I told him that there is no hope for me, and that really angered me. Why would a total stranger care for me? Why would someone who I caused him immense pain, by slaying those he loved, care for me? Why does he care for me? I screamed with all my might. I was desperate. Nothing of the sort had ever happened to me.

Then he stopped in his tracks. I did too. He surprised me. Then he took a few steps and showed me something. It was a beautiful Ethereal Flower with violet coloured petals. I never saw it before. He told me that it was the one he was searching for. It would save his friend.

I stammered. I asked him about the other three he picked. When I did, tears rained down from his eyes, and he said that he didn't want to do this, but I gave him no other choice. Not that he was wrong...

Then he took them out, and he whispered something. Something I didn't understand. Then the three flowers were in my hands, and a pink whirlwind blew and sucked me in. Before I was completely sucked in, my eyes fell on Hades for one last time. I saw him falling on his knees saying, "I'm sorry" with tears still flowing from his eyes.

That is my story until now. Now I'm in a place where I can't do anything. A place of exile, a place of punishment; not that I don't deserve it, of course. But I think that my time has come again. I've stayed here for far too long.

You see, the villagers and the town's people have all forgotten about me, about my very existence. And I must do something about it, don't you think? I must remind them who I am and what I've done, for I am Globalea the Queen of the Grandea Forest, or else known as Golden Woods, and the Queen of the White Mist Mountain.

It's time for my return. Get ready!